returned on or b..
te stamped bei.

THIS WALKER BOOK BELONGS TO:

This book is dedicated to the memory of Ben,
a boy who loved animals

First published 1990 by
Walker Books Ltd, 87 Vauxhall Walk
London SE11 5HJ

This edition published 1992

6 8 10 9 7

© 1990 Sarah Hayes

Printed in Hong Kong/China

British Library Cataloguing in Publication Data
A catalogue record for this book is
available from the British Library.

ISBN 0-7445-2018-5

Nine Ducks Nine

Written and illustrated by

Sarah Hayes

WALKER BOOKS
AND SUBSIDIARIES
LONDON • BOSTON • SYDNEY

Nine ducks nine walked out in line.

Mr Fox was watching.

One duck ran away,

down to the rickety bridge.

We'll get that fox

Eight ducks eight sat on the gate.

Mr Fox came through the woods.

One duck ran away,

down to the rickety bridge.

Seven ducks seven took off together.

Mr Fox came out of the woods.

One duck flew away,

down to the rickety bridge.

We have a plan

Six ducks six did balancing tricks.

Mr Fox came closer.

One duck ran away,

down to the rickety bridge.

Yoo-hoo, Foxy

Five ducks five began to dive.

Mr Fox came closer.

One duck swam away,

down to the rickety bridge.

Four ducks four reached the shore.

Mr Fox came closer and closer.

One duck flew away,

down to the rickety bridge.

Foxes can
swim

Three ducks three flew into a tree.

Mr Fox came closer and closer.

One duck flew away,

down to the rickety bridge.

Two ducks two had things to do.

Mr Fox came even closer.

One duck crept away,

to the end of the rickety bridge.

One duck one sat in the sun,
all alone on the rickety bridge.
Mr Fox came right up close and…

Mr Fox pounced!

Come here

The rickety bridge broke and
SPLASH!
Mr Fox fell into the river.

Nine ducks nine swam back in line.
Mr Fox went home to his den
and never chased those ducks again.

MORE WALKER PAPERBACKS
For You to Enjoy

Also by Sarah Hayes

THIS IS THE BEAR
THIS IS THE BEAR AND THE PICNIC LUNCH
THIS IS THE BEAR AND THE SCARY NIGHT
THIS IS THE BEAR AND THE BAD LITTLE GIRL
illustrated by Helen Craig

Four rollicking cumulative rhymes about a boy, a dog and a bear.

"For those ready for their first story, there could be no better choice…
Helen Craig's pictures are just right." *Judy Taylor, The Independent*

0-7445-0969-6   *This Is the Bear*   £4.99
0-7445-1304-9   *This Is the Bear and the Picnic Lunch*   £4.99
0-7445-3147-0   *This Is the Bear and the Scary Night*   £4.99
0-7445-4771-7   *This Is the Bear and the Bad Little Girl*   £4.99

MARY MARY
illustrated by Helen Craig

A contrary girl meets and sorts out a ramshackle giant.

"Helen Craig's pictures of the giant are just right." *The Teacher*

0-7445-2062-2   £4.99

THE GRUMPALUMP
illustrated by Barbara Firth

Just what is the grumpalump? A mole can roll on it, a dove can shove it, a yak can whack it
and an armadillo can use it for a pillow. But what is it, and why is it so grumpy?

"Jauntily drawn and painted… Irresistible, easy-to-read fantasy." *The Observer*

0-7445-2021-5   £5.99